This

Ladybird First Favourite Tale

belongs to

...Jessica...

Published by Ladybird Books Ltd
A Penguin Company
Penguin Books Ltd, 80 Strand, London WC2R 0RL, UK
Penguin Books Australia Ltd, Camberwell, Victoria, Australia
Penguin Group (NZ) 67 Apollo Drive, Rosedale, North Shore 0632, New Zealand

001 – 10 9 8 7 6 5 4 3 2 1

© Ladybird Books Ltd MCMXCIX
This edition MMXII

ISBN: 978-1-40930-955-0

Printed in China

Ladybird First Favourite Tales

The Sly FOX and the Little Red Hen

BASED ON A TRADITIONAL FOLK TALE
retold by Mandy Ross ★ illustrated by Jan Lewis

Once there was a little red hen. She lived in a little red henhouse, safe and sound, with a little blue door and windows all around.

She was a happy hen. Every day she searched for grain with a peck, peck, peck and a cluck, cluck, cluck. But then . . .

...a sly young fox and his mother moved into a nearby den.

The sly fox was always hungry. He licked his lips when he saw the little red hen searching for grain with a peck, peck, peck and a cluck, cluck, cluck. And then . . .

...the sly fox tried to catch the little red hen. He plotted and planned, again and again.

But the little red hen was clever.
She always got away, with a peck, peck, peck
and a cluck, cluck, cluck. But then ...

...the sly fox thought up a very sly plan.
"Mother, boil some water in a pan," he said.
"I'll bring home supper tonight."

Then he crept over to the little red henhouse.
And he waited ...

...until at last the little red hen came out to search for grain with a peck, peck, peck and a cluck, cluck, cluck.

Quick as a flash, the sly fox
slipped into the henhouse.
And he waited ...

...until the little red hen came hurrying home.
As soon as she saw the fox, she flew up to
the rafters.
"You can't catch me now!" she laughed, with
a peck, peck, peck and a cluck, cluck, cluck.

"All part of my plan," smiled the fox on the ground. And slowly he started to chase his tail, round and round ...

...and round and round, faster and faster ...
until the little red hen up in the rafters
grew dizzy.

"Oh!" she clucked. "My poor head's spinning.
I'm all in a tizzy." And she dropped down –
plop! – straight into the fox's sack.
"Ha!" laughed the fox. And then ...

...the fox slung the sack over his shoulder and set off for home with the little red hen.

After a while, he stopped for a rest. The sun was warm and soon he was snoozing. "Now's my chance," whispered the little red hen, and out she crept *without* a peck, peck, peck or a cluck, cluck, cluck.

Quickly she rolled some large stones into the sack and tied a knot at the top.

Then she ran all the way home and didn't stop till she was safe in her little red henhouse.

The fox woke up and went on his way, hungry for his supper.

"This hen is heavy!" he said to himself, licking his lips. "She'll make a good meal."

"Is the pot boiling, Mother?" he called at the den.
"Look who I've got! It's the little red hen."
"Throw her in, son," said his mother.
"She'll make a nice snack."

So the sly fox opened up the sack.
Into the boiling water crashed the
stones with a SPLASH!
And that was the end of the sly fox
and his mother.

And the little red hen lived happily ever
after in her little red henhouse, searching
for grain with a peck, peck, peck and
a cluck, cluck, cluck.